Catching Fish

and

Other Stories

Other titles in this series

Kalo and the Koel and Other Stories

Kalo is a young village lad, who loves the world of nature around him. One day he captures a bird, but then, sympathizing with her longing for freedom, sets her free, and befriends her. The close friendship between the boy and the koel is tested by a long, enforced separation, but finally the friends are reunited. In 'Drawing Pictures' a group of poor children take up colours and paper left lying around after a sit and draw competition for privileged children, and find that the experience of creativity allows them to soar free.

ISBN 81 7046 154 5 Rs 85

Little Flower Shefali and Other Stories

'Somewhere . . .' is a lullaby in prose, a delightful little tale about a child who pesters his sleepy aunt for a story, only to fall asleep himself before the end. Shefali is a little girl who is put out to work as a maid by her parents, who cannot afford to feed her. She starts to learn how to read and write, facing ridicule and gradually overcoming her inhibitions by coming to terms with her own inner creativity. In 'Their Friend the Smoke Person' a brother and sister befriend a mysterious stranger, a 'smoke person' who appears and disappears at will.

ISBN 81 7046 179 0 Rs 95

Catching Fish

and Other Stories

Written and Illustrated by

Meera Mukherjee

Translated by

Anjum Katyal

Seagull Books
CALCUTTA 2000

Designed by Naveen Kishore

ISBN 81 7046 180 4

Published by Naveen Kishore
Seagull Books Private Limited, 26 Circus Avenue, Calcutta 700 017, India

Processed by Jasra Graphics Private Limited,
Unit One, First Floor, Prabhadevi Industrial Estate,
408, Veer Savarkar Marg, Prabhadevi, Mumbai 400 025
Printed in India by Pragati Art Printers,
17, Red Hills, Hyderabad 500 004

Contents

Catching Fish

One monsoon season, an amazing amount of water collected, turning overgrown ponds and puddles into one big pool. Fish from the ponds were spilling over, jumping about everywhere, here a koi fish, there a parshey. And grownups were busy catching them—using their hands, sieves and nets of different kinds, whatever they could find.

Amidst all this Madhu, Radhu and Rahup were squatting beside a tiny pool, using small pieces of mosquito netting to try and catch some fish, too.

All three of them were using the same thing to catch fish with.

Their faces were reflected in the water. Suddenly Madhu caught hold of Radhu's ear and twisted it hard. Radhu yelled, 'Why did you twist my ear?! I'm going to twist yours!' Madhu said, 'I couldn't make out in the water whose ear it was. So I twisted it, and I saw that it was yours, not mine.'

Radhu looked at the water and said, 'That's true, it's all getting mixed up in the reflection. You can't make out which hand belongs to whom. You can make out the faces, though. The head of hair that looks like a mop is Madhu's.' Madhu immediately shouted, 'And the hair that looks like a clump of grass is yours!'

Rahup said, 'While you two waste your time fighting, the fish are getting a chance to escape.'

Radhu said, 'Me, fighting? It's Madhu who's fighting.'

Madhu said, 'Why did you say that my

hair was like a mop?' He continued, annoyed. 'Look here, I have the power to burn

alive people if I get really angry.'

Radhu got even more angry. He dropped the net and stood up. 'Go ahead. I'm standing right here.

Show me what you can do.'

Madhu also got to his feet and stood staring hard at Radhu, eyes stretched wide. After some time he asked, 'Aren't you feeling hot?'

Radhu replied, 'Not in the least bit.'

Madhu hugged Radhu and said, 'You're my friend. That's why it isn't working on you.'

Rahup
said, 'Are
you two
going to
keep
fighting?
See how
many
punti fish
I've man-
aged to
catch!'

A little
ashamed,
Madhu
and
Radhu
sat down.

Suddenly,

an amazingly

large fish

entered

their
net.

But their mosquito netting wasn't big enough, and the fish turned around and went back into the water. They could clearly see the fish between their three heads and six hands. The shadow of the fish mingled with theirs. Radhu said, 'We can't tell our shadows apart. Do you think that the fish can make out that its shadow has got mixed up with ours?'

Madhu said, 'We must catch that fish. I feel it's related to us, somehow–an aunt, perhaps, or an uncle.'

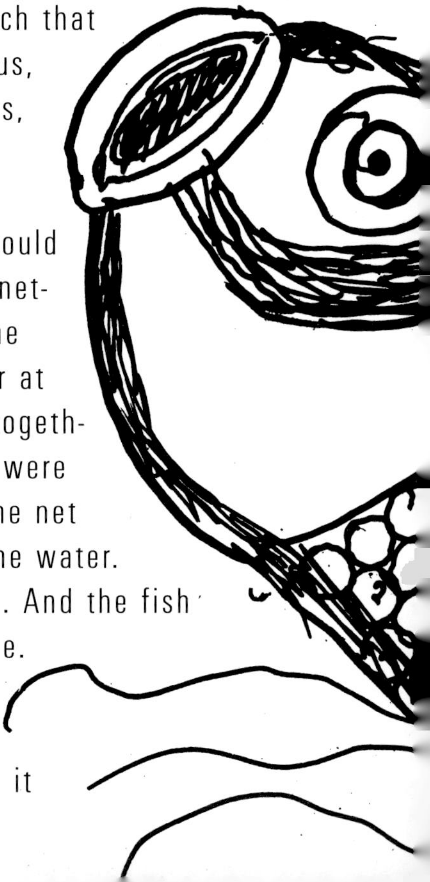

They made a plan. They would tie their bits of mosquito netting together and throw the whole thing into the water at one go. The three pieces together made a huge net. They were very happy. They swung the net around and flung it into the water. Now it was the fish's turn. And the fish came, but after a long time.

This time it looked as if it was all dressed up. And it

seemed much bigger than before.

It entered their net, and didn't swim out again. But it was such a heavy fish that even when all three of them heaved together, with all their strength, they couldn't lift it out.

As they strained and grunted, they suddenly felt as if the fish was trying to speak to them. They quickly pricked up their ears and sat still.

They heard an
amazing thing. The fish was really talking!

It was saying, 'Look, if you
stop fighting, I'll
come
to you.
If you
love me, I'll
love you too. I'll be your friend. Do
you eat your friends? We fish
don't eat our friends.'

They sat as if stunned, amazed, listening to the fish speak. They stared and stared, and then, feeling as if the sky was calling to them, they looked up—and saw that the huge shadow of the fish was lying across the sky as well! They looked down at the water, then up at the sky.

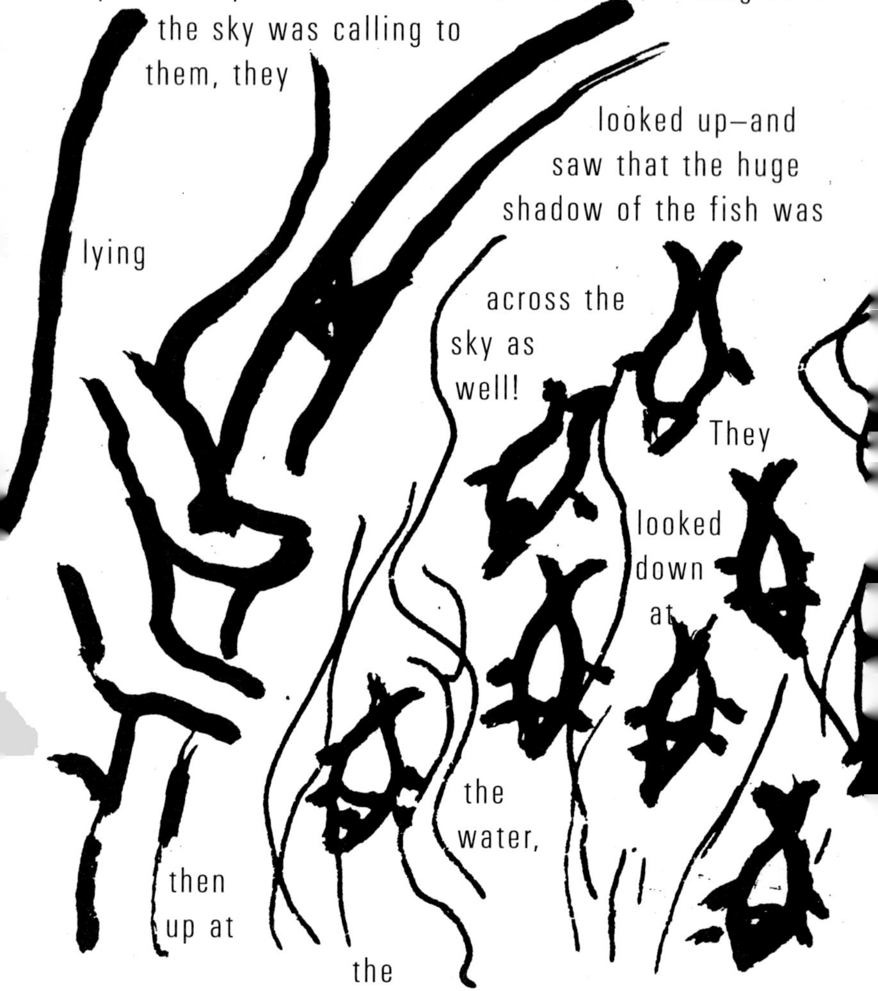

The fish began to speak again. 'Come on, promise me you won't fight again. Will you?' All three boys spoke together, 'We promise, we won't ever fight again.'

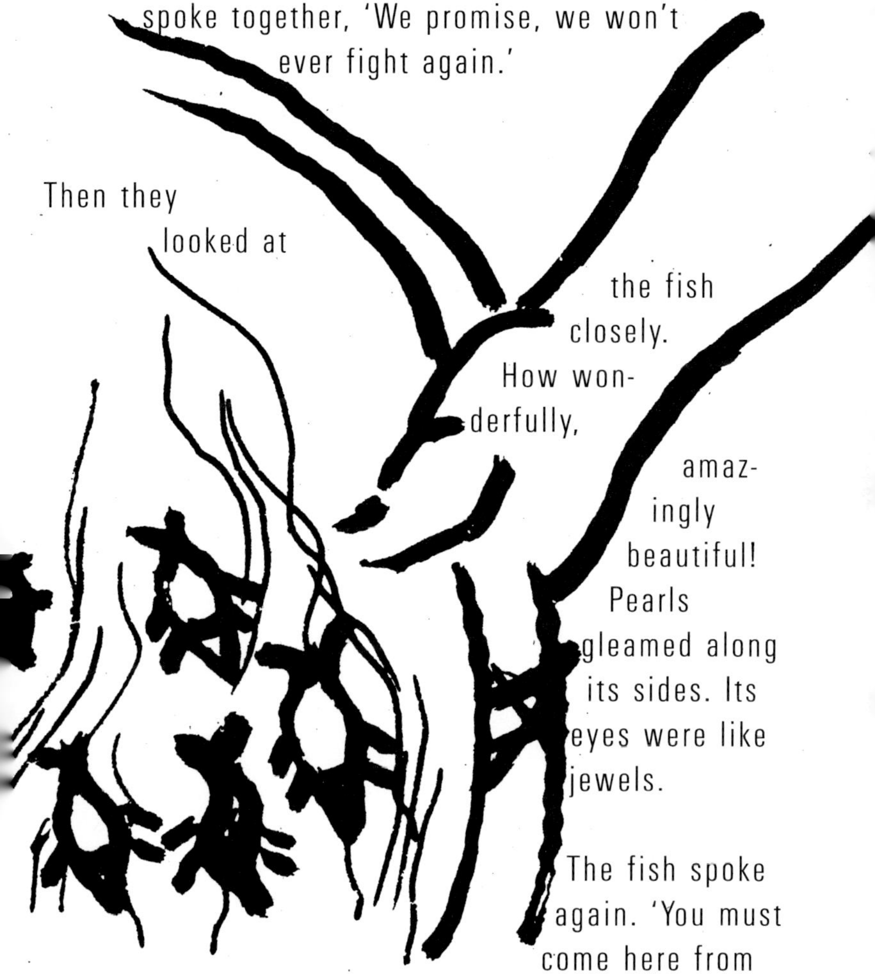

Then they looked at the fish closely. How wonderfully, amazingly beautiful! Pearls gleamed along its sides. Its eyes were like jewels.

The fish spoke again. 'You must come here from time to time. We'll chat and play together.'

Saying
this,
the fish

vanished.

The three boys got up. Rahup released all the little fish he had caught, freeing them in the water before he went home.

Quilt

Mother said, 'Just call one of the cotton carders, will you? Look, there they are!' Khoka went running up, hopping and skipping happily, calling out, 'Oh cotton carder! Hey, cotton carder!'

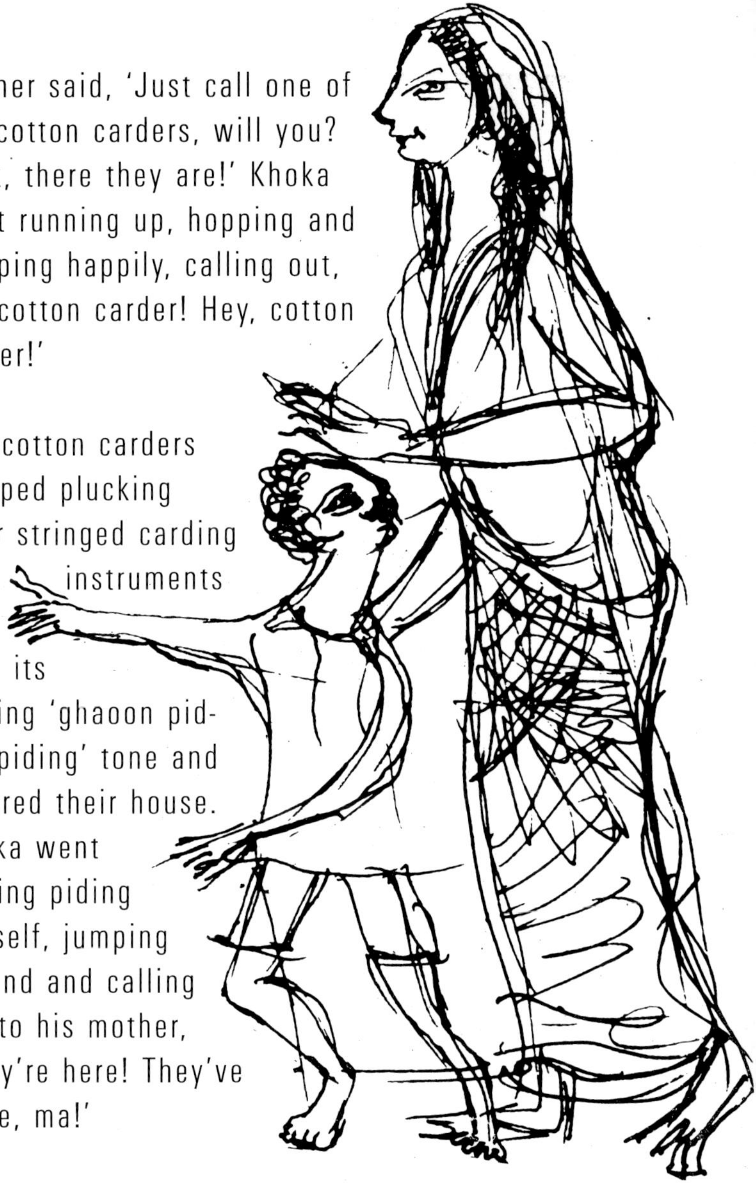

The cotton carders stopped plucking their stringed carding instruments with its ringing 'ghaoon pid-ing piding' tone and entered their house. Khoka went thiding piding himself, jumping around and calling out to his mother, 'They're here! They've come, ma!'

Mother went at once to take out the old quilt from Bandipota and said, 'Look here, baba, from this quilt I want you to make me two small quilts.' The carders looked grave, and through their reddened, blackened paan-chewing teeth they said, 'There isn't enough cotton for that, ma. You'll need some more cotton.'

'Oh dear!' said Mother. 'I don't have any more cotton, baba. Can't you manage with this much?'

They scratched their heads helplessly, and then said, 'Achchha, we'll do it. We have some cotton with us.'

They settled the rate with Mother, and then they set to work. She went indoors, and the boy squatted down beside them to watch them working.

The boy watched them as they started combing and fluffing out the cotton. Then they began filling two quilts with the fluffy cotton. Khoka clearly saw them stuff one quilt half full, and the other only a quarter full. As he wondered, now what'll they do, an amazing thing happened! One by one the two of them stretched their arms up towards the sky!

Autumn. The sky was blue. It was filling up with fluffy cotton-white clouds. The carders were stuffing the quilts with these clouds. Eyes round with wonder, Khoka asked, 'And what if it starts raining inside the quilts?!'

The cotton carders said, 'Silly boy! Only rainclouds bring rain. These fluffy clouds are just like cotton.' They added, 'Do you want to see something, Khoka babu? Shall we show you something wonderful?' He said, 'What?'

'We can stitch the clouds into quilts and covers for the living creatures of the sky.'

Khoka said, 'You mean for the birds? But they live in trees.' The carders replied, 'No. There are creatures you cannot see with your eyes. They are made of clouds. For example, there are cloud people, cloud elephants, cloud horses, and lots of other such creatures. In winter we have to make quilts for them.'

Khoka was dancing with excitement. 'Yes, yes, I want to see them! Please show them to me just once, please!'

The carders said, 'Then come on, let's go.'

Riding on the older carder's shoulders,

Khoka began to rise up into the sky, and saw how the carders were stitching the clouds in a hundred different ways.

They fluffed and combed them out as they flew along. But those cloud quilts were nothing like ours. Some went from long to fat, others from thin to round, yet others started off aslant and became square, and what not!

Then it was meeting time. The carders started plucking tunes from their instruments. Such were the notes they sounded that first a cloud elephant arrived, next a flat looking horse, then a human being with a squished-up face. They all said, 'Now what do you want? We give you rain, don't we?'

The carders said, 'We aren't farmers who can make use of your rainfall.'
The cloud army asked,

'Why? Isn't the cotton tree useful to you?'

The carders said, 'Yes, of course it is. But we still have to buy cotton in the market. The money for that?'

The clouds held a meeting and said, 'Our money isn't the same as human money. You won't be able to use it there. Instead of that, we offer you as much white cloud cotton as you like from the autumn skies.'

Khoka was very worried, 'But if you fill the quilts with clouds, it will rain inside the quilts!'

The clouds answered, 'Even if it does rain, the cloud cotton will be such that it'll dry in a second.'

Khoka felt comforted.

After
this the
carders
dropped
Khoka
home
and
went
away.

Ever since then, whenever Khoka hears the ghaaon piding piding sound the carders make, he runs out of his house, but he has never seen them again. He looks for them up in the sky. But autumn comes and goes, and still he doesn't catch sight of them.

Sometimes he thinks of them
and won-
ders if they
are busy
stitching
quilts in the
clouds,
quilts for
the cloud
elephants,
the flat
cloud people
and all the
other amaz-
ing creatures
of the skies.

Growing Up

Look at
the long
line of
children
walking
along the
path! Boys
and girls,
mothers
and grand-
mothers,
everyone
is off to
the village
fair.

What a crowd of stands and stalls! Look, there are kite stalls, stands selling little clay toys, and piles upon piles of low tables and stools. But the shops the little children like the best are the ones selling small tin toys wrapped in twists of colourful cellophane. There are tiny little stoves, pots and pans, ladles, rolling pins and lanterns. They love these the most. Apart from this, there are hawkers selling clothes, containers for grain, winnowing trays, knives and sickles. And, of course, there are hundreds of food stalls!

Nilu and Purnima buy a set of cellophane-wrapped utensils each. They make four-anna offerings at the shrines of a muslim gazi and the goddess, Sitala ma. Then they pester their grandmother into treating them to fresh, hot fritters and sweet jalebis. Now it's time to go home. Ma remembers to gather up everything she has bought—a container for grain, a winnowing tray, a stool, a pitcher—and not leave anything behind. Purnima remembers her doll's utensils, and Nilu her toys, her doll, and a tiny clay pitcher.

Walking along behind their mother and grandmother, they chat gaily about all sorts of things—about one marrying her daughter off to the other's son, the dishes they'll cook for the wedding feast and goodness knows what else.

For Nilu and Purnima, life flows on in this way. While their mother works in the field, they cook for the family. One day, while straining away the boiling hot rice water, Nilu's leg gets scalded. What an uproar! Scurrying about, Purnima gets together some oil and salt to soothe the burn. She rushes across to the neighbouring hut. The old grandmother, who's at home, makes a paste with the oil, salt and some herbs, and rubs it on the wounded leg. Finally, Nilu's yells and screams quieten down.

In the mango season, they sneak away the delicious fruit, and feast on the pickle they make from it. In the hot afternoons, while everyone's asleep, they sit by the bank of the pond and spend hours watching the widening ripples on the surface of the water.

The other day they were playing at cooking. They had gathered the stalks and shoots of some wayside weeds and were busy cooking fish, chopping, stirring and frying. A group of boys and girls gathered, but the two friends were totally absorbed in their work. They had set their minds on the job before them, and they carried on and on and on . . .

Suddenly it seems that a long, long time has passed. They're no longer little girls. Nilu and Purnima stare at each other in stunned silence. When did they stop playing with dolls, when did they turn into dolls themselves? They can't understand it. They look down at themselves, at each other. Wrapped in handwoven saris, heads demurely covered, feet outlined with red alta, rings piercing their noses. Red dots of sindoor on their foreheads, red sindoor in the parting of their hair.

With wide-open, unblinking eyes they sit, each staring at the other without saying a word.